THE Grossery GANG

YOUR SHOPPIN'S GONE ROTTEN!

A Cheap Treats Halloween!

BuzzPop

Halloween was Puking Pumpkin's favorite day of the year!

"I can't wait to celebrate with gross costumes and moldy candy!" he said.

But first he had to find friends to go trick-or-treating with him.

Just then, Flat Battery appeared dressed as Frankenstein's monster.

"Are you going trick-or-treating?" asked Surge.

"Of course!" said Puking Pumpkin. "I've been rotting all year for this! Let's find some others to join us."

As the pair walked down the vile aisles, they spotted Putrid Pizza.

"Spooky costume, Pizza Face!" called Puking Pumpkin. "Do you want to come trick-or-treating with us?"

"Only if you wear a scary costume!" said Pizza Face. "You won't get any treats looking like a friendly neighborhood gourd."

At that moment, Dodgey Donut crashed into them.

"Hey, Rocky!" said Puking Pumpkin. "What are you dressed as, a lunch lady?"

"These are spiderwebs, not hairnets!" said Rocky. "Is there anything scarier than spiders? They're bugs that eat other bugs!"

That gave Puking Pumpkin an idea. He went to put on a really scary costume.

"Nice vampire costume," said Surge when Puking Pumpkin returned.

"Thanks," said Puking Pumpkin. "Okay, Scream Team. Let's get all the treats in the Yucky Mart!"

"Listen!" said Rocky. "Wha-wha-what's that sound?"

Just then, MP Flea Player appeared, blasting the spookiest music.

"That music will scare even the bravest of the Grossery Gang!" Pizza Face said with a laugh.

"If you need tunes, I'm your goon," said MP Flea Player. The gang set off to trick-or-treat.

First the Scream Team visited Blue Spew Cheese.

"Trick or treat!" they shouted.

They expected to get tons of treats. Instead, Stinky let out a cloud of foul gas and fainted.

"Weird, I guess the old dude needed a nap!" said Pizza Face. "Gross dreams, Stinky!"

Next the Scream Team found Grub Sub rummaging through the lost and found looking for candy.

The gang surrounded him and yelled, "Trick or treat!"

Meathead didn't recognize his friends in their scary costumes. "Ah! You'll never get me alive, you maggot-eaten monsters!" he shouted, launching garbage at the Scream Team.

"He's lost his meatballs! Everyone, make like a nose and run!" screamed Surge.

The gang ran straight into Sewer Glove. They startled Fingers so bad, he flung all of his candy into the air. It rattled away into air vents. Fingers leapt so high, he got stuck on the ceiling fan.

"This is rotten!" complained Puking Pumpkin. "We haven't gotten any treats! Everyone is too scared of us."

"Let's try Shoccoli," said Rocky. "He isn't scared of anything."

The Scream Team found Doc Brocc. "Trick or treat!" they yelled. To their surprise, Doc Brocc was not impressed.

"You call those costumes scary? No way! You're not even getting a maggot from me," he told them. "And don't come back for any tricks or treats. I'm going to sleep. GOOD NIGHT!"

"Halloween is ruined," said Puking Pumpkin.

"No, it's not," said Pizza Face. "Since Doc Brocc won't give us treats, we get to play a trick on him!"

So Puking Pumpkin and his friends thought of a plan. They arranged themselves in the shape of a big scary ghost. Then they went back to find Doc Brocc, who was now sleeping in the bakery.

"MP Flea Player, go hit the lights," whispered Pizza Face.

Very carefully, the big scary ghost crept up to Doc Brocc's shadow.

"BOO!" they shouted.

When nothing happened, the Scream Team was confused. "Rise and rot, Doc!" said Puking Pumpkin.

The Scream Team took off their ghost costume. MP Flea Player turned on the lights.

"Ahhhh!" the Scream Team bellowed from the depths of their bellies.

The Scream Team was face-to-face
with terrifying creatures!

"Ooooh . . ." the monsters moaned.

One of the creatures started to move.

"Gotcha!" it said. It was Doc Brocc! He laughed and pulled off his Halloween mask.

"Doc! We thought you were asleep," cried Rocky.

"That was just a moldy baguette," he said.

"What a nasty trick," said Puking Pumpkin.

"In Cheap Town, tricks ARE treats!" Doc Brocc said.

One by one, the scary creatures revealed themselves.

"It's you!" cried Rocky as Stinky, Meathead, and Fingers all removed their Halloween costumes.

"You got us, so we got you!" said Stinky.

"We couldn't leave you hanging," added Fingers.

Puking Pumpkin and the other trick-or-treaters all started to laugh.

"That was an awesomely rotten trick!" cried Pizza Face.

"I was so scared that I almost puked my pants!" said Puking Pumpkin.

"Now that we've had our Halloween trick, let's have some treats!" said Doc Brocc.

Fingers shared the candy he had retrieved from the air vents.

"I found this moldy candy in the lost and found!" said Meathead.

"Sweet!" cried the rest of the Grossery Gang.